SMART ABOUT
Art

CLAUDE MONET
Sunshine and Waterlilies

Written and illustrated by
True Kelley

Grosset & Dunlap • New York

To Charlotte and Eloise Lindblom—T.K.

Cover: *La Grenouillère*, by Claude Monet. The Metropolitan Museum of Art, H.O. Havemeyer Collection, Bequest of Mrs. H.O. Havemeyer, 1929. (29.100.112) Photograph © 1989 The Metropolitan Museum of Art

Library of Congress Cataloging-in-Publication Data

Kelley, True.
    Claude Monet : sunshine and waterlilies / written and illustrated by True Kelley.
        p. cm.
    Written as a report by a fictitious student.
    1. Monet, Claude, 1840–1926—Juvenile literature. 2. Painters—France—Biography—Juvenile literature. [1. Monet, Claude, 1840–1926. 2. Artists.] I. Title.

    ND553.M7   K445   2001
    759.4—dc21
    [B]   2001023147

ISBN 0-448-42522-X (pbk)   A B C D E F G H I J
ISBN 0-448-42613-7 (GB)   A B C D E F G H I J

From the desk of
Ms. Brandt

Dear Class,

Our unit on famous artists is almost over. I hope that you enjoyed it as much as I did.

I am excited to read your reports. Here are some questions that you may want to think about:

- Why did you pick your artist?

- If you could ask your artist 3 questions, what would they be?

- Did you learn anything that really surprised you?

Good luck and have fun!

Ms. Brandt

Last year I visited my grandma in Boston, and she took me to the art museum. She wanted to show me something that she had shown my dad when he was my age. She told me to close my eyes. Grandma led me by the hand and then told me to open my eyes.

This is what I saw:

Blobs of paint!

Detail of *Rouen Cathedral Façade and Tour d'Albane (Morning Effect)*, by Claude Monet. 1894. Courtesy, Museum of Fine Arts, Boston. Reproduced with permission. © 2000 Museum of Fine Arts, Boston. All Rights Reserved.

I was standing very very close to a painting. Then Grandma told me to back up. I was so surprised!

Rouen Cathedral Façade and Tour d'Albane (Morning Effect), by Claude Monet. 1894. Courtesy, Museum of Fine Arts, Boston. Reproduced with permission. © 2000 Museum of Fine Arts, Boston. All Rights Reserved.

Now the paint blobs turned into a big, beautiful picture of a cathedral. An artist named Claude Monet painted it in 1894. How could he paint the picture standing up so close? Then I saw other paintings he did—waterlilies and rivers and trains (trains are cool!). I liked them all. That's why I picked Claude Monet for my report.

The Young Cartoonist

Oscar-Claude Monet (Moe-nay) was born in France on November 14, 1840. His dad was a grocer.

Claude didn't like school much. In grade school he started doing funny drawings of his teachers and selling them to his classmates.

In high school Claude drew boats and people in his town. For a 16 year-old kid, he was good!

Mario Orchard, by Claude Monet. Gift of Mr and Mrs. Carter H. Harrison, 1933.891. Photograph courtesy of The Art Institute of Chicago.

WOW!

I tried this, but nobody would pay even 25 cents!

When his mom died, Claude quit school. His aunt took care of him. She was a painter, and she wanted Claude to be an artist. But Claude's father wanted him to be a grocer just like he was.

Monet, the Student

Photo of Claude Monet, Cliché Bibliothèque Nationale de France, Paris.

← Here's "Dandy" Monet when he got to Paris. Check out the necktie!

When Claude was 18 years old, he went to Paris to study painting even though his dad was against it. But Claude didn't like the art school much. It taught kind of an old-fashioned way of painting. Also, most artists in those days painted indoors, but Claude liked to paint outdoors.

Claude became good friends with other painters in Paris: Auguste Renoir, Alfred Sisley, and Frederic Bazille. Their nickname for Claude was "Dandy" because, even though he was broke, he still wore shirts with ruffled cuffs.

Monet   DANDY!   Bazille   Sisley   Renoir

Claude and his friends were all very interested in how light changes the way you see things. They went on painting trips outside Paris.

Here's a painting Monet did when he was 25.

Pointe de la Hève at Low Tide, by Claude Monet. 1865. Kimbell Art Museum, Fort Worth, Texas

None of them had any money. All they cared about was painting. They once lived on beans for two months straight. I thought school lunch was bad!

The Salon (not a beauty parlor)

In those days, there was a big painting show in Paris called the Salon. If artists got their paintings accepted into the Salon, they could sell them. If they didn't, they were out of luck. The Salon artists painted things the way they thought they should look. And they thought things should look pretty.

This is a Salon painting,→ Kinda boring.

Evening or Lost Illusions, by Charles Gleyre. Réunion des Musées Nationaux/Art Resource, NY

Claude and his friends were painting in a new way. They tried to paint exactly what they saw on the spot.

Claude started a big painting called *Women in the Garden*. He painted outdoors and waited for the light to be right to paint. He dug a trench and used a pulley system to lower the painting so he could paint the top part.

Some paint colors Monet used

cadmium yellow   yellow ochre   viridian   vermilion   cobalt blue   cobalt violet   black   white

Women in the Garden at Ville d'Avray, by Claude Monet. Photo: Herve Lewandowski. Réunion des Musées Nationaux/Art Resource, NY

Monet's girlfriend Camille posed for all the women in the picture.

Did the Salon take his painting after all that work? No! They rejected it. But there's no way he'd stop painting! Even on cold, snowy days he kept painting outdoors, with blankets and a hot water bottle and wearing three overcoats!

The Frog Pond

It was hard to swim in those outfits!

For a while Claude, Camille, and their baby Jean lived near Claude's painter friend Auguste Renoir. They were so poor, Renoir gave the Monet family gifts of food.

In the summer, Claude and Renoir painted together. They both painted *La Grenouillère*. That means "the Frog Pond" in French. It was a popular place to swim.

This is Monet's.

La Grenouillère, by Claude Monet. The Metropolitan Museum of Art, H.O. Havemeyer Collection, bequest of Mrs. H.O. Havemeyer, 1929. (29.100.112)
Photograph © 1989 The Metropolitan Museum of Art.

Renoir's painting is soft, and Monet's is kind of zippy. I like Monet's painting better. I can imagine what it was really like at the frog pond more than I can from Renoir's painting. Renoir seems more interested in painting the people and their clothes. Monet tries to paint the feeling of the whole place.

This is Renoir's.

La Grenouillère, by Auguste Renoir. The National Museum of Fine Art, Stockholm

The Rejects Show

In 1863, the Salon rejected so many good paintings that Monet and other artists decided to forget the Salon and set up their own show called the Salon de Refusés. In English that means "the Rejects Show." People who saw the show made fun of it.

Here's a picture of Camille and Jean in a poppy field. I can't see why anyone wouldn't like it.

The Poppy Field, near Argenteuil, by Claude Monet. Musee d'Orsay. Photo: Herve Lewandowski. Réunion des Musées Nationaux/Art Resource, NY

In 1874, Claude and his friends held another show. Most people thought this show was a big joke, too. Claude showed his painting *Impression: Sunrise*. That was where the name "Impressionism" came from.

Impression, Sunrise, by Claude Monet. 1872. Erich Lessing/Art Resource, NY.

Impressionism is a style of painting that tries to get the look and feel of a scene right at the moment it was painted. So a whole art style got named because of one Monet picture. How cool is that?

The Studio Boat

Claude was really getting into painting water, even though the Seine River was horribly polluted. He made a floating studio out of a small boat. He could sit inside or outside and paint.

Camille went with Monet a lot.

★ This Is My Favorite! ★

Ever since I took a train to Boston, I love trains!

Claude liked to paint the same things over and over. He painted this Paris train station twelve times. He got the stationmaster to stop trains and close off platforms for him. They even would fire up the locomotives so they made lots of steam for Claude to paint.

Monet's Big Family

Claude and Camille had another son, Michel. They still had no money. They had to move in with their friends Alice and Ernest Hoschedes and their six children. Monet didn't even have money for paints and brushes. He needed a lot of paint. He did 300 paintings that year!

The Monet and Hoschedes Family

All in One House

Camille

Monet

Alice

Ernest

They need a dog.

Marthe

Suzanne

Blanche

Germaine

Jacques

Jean

Jean-Pierre

Michel

Then Camille got really sick. She was only 32 years old when she died. What a terrible time! Claude was so sad. Some of the other paintings he did after Camille died look sad, too.

Monet painted this picture of Camille right after she died. It's creepy, but I can't stop looking at it.

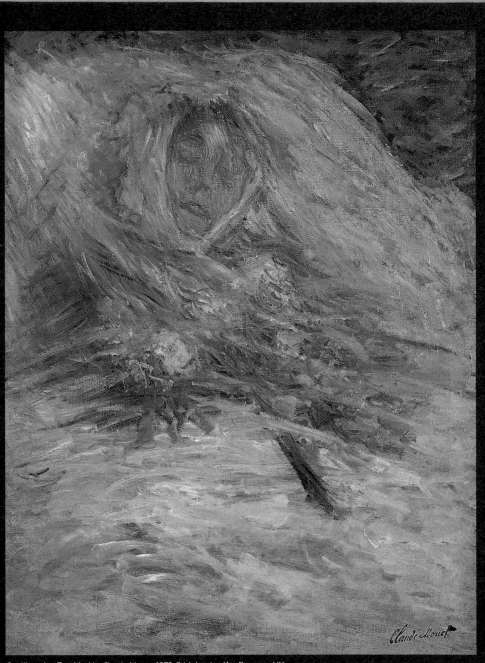

Camille on her Deathbed, by Claude Monet. 1879. Erich Lessing/Art Resource, NY

Better Times

But finally Claude's luck began to change. By 1880, his paintings were starting to sell. People were beginning to like Claude's art and the Impressionist style.

Claude began taking long trips to paint faraway places. He went to Italy with his old friend Auguste Renoir. Monet painted with different colors—ones he had never used before. That's because things really looked different in Italy.

Villas à Bordighera, by Claude Monet. 1884. Santa Barbara Museum of Art, Bequest of Katherine Dexter McCormick in memory of her husband, Stanley McCormick.

ultramarine turquoise pink orange

← These are some of the colors Monet was using now!

Claude liked to imagine being born blind and then suddenly being able to see. He tried to paint things as if he were seeing them for the very first time.

Sometimes Claude got mad at a painting because it wasn't working out. He had a bad temper. Once he kicked a hole in his canvas, and another time he was working on his boat and threw all his art supplies into the river! I know how he felt, believe me. Sometimes I hate how my pictures come out and would like to rip them up.

Fame At Last!

Now Claude was getting famous. In 1890, he bought a pink house in Giverny. He married his old friend Alice Hoschedes. He had lived with her for over 10 years, so it was about time. He hired two cooks and six gardeners. He had them plant lots of irises, because they were his favorite. He also built a waterlily pond with a little bridge over it. His kids liked to catch frogs, row boats, swim, and fish.

Claude Monet in his garden at Giverny. Mary Evans Picture Library

Portrait of Monet. © Roger-Viollet, Paris

I follow nature but I cannot catch her.

Claude was in his sixties and still painting things again and again at different times of the day and in different weather.

He painted wheat stacks and trees. He spent three years painting pictures of a cathedral. One of them is the painting my grandma showed me.

Here are two pictures I took of the same place on different days.

Rainy Day

← My dad

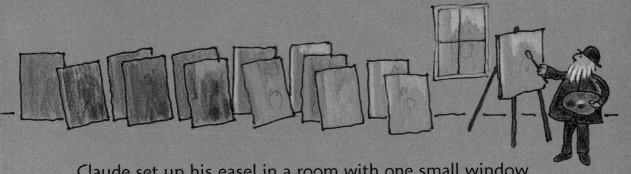

Claude set up his easel in a room with one small window across from the cathedral. He was working on fourteen paintings of the cathedral on the same day. He changed canvases almost every half hour, whenever the light changed. In the morning the cathedral looked misty blue. By evening sunset it was orange and blue. On rainy days, the cathedral looked gray. By the time he was all finished, Claude was sick of the cathedral. He had nightmares that it was falling on top of him.

These pictures look like different places... but only the light has changed!

Sunny Day

This would make a nice painting!

Waterlilies

waterlily bud

Even after Claude Monet was famous, and you'd think he could relax, he still kept painting like mad. But his life became more peaceful. He worked more at home. He sat under a white umbrella and painted water that reflected the clouds and grasses on the edge of his pond at Giverny.

Monet and the bridge in the garden of Giverny. © Roger-Viollet, Paris

Here's Monet standing in his water garden. No wonder he liked to paint it!

Water Lilies, by Claude Monet. 1916. Matsukata Collection, The National Museum of Western Art, Tokyo

Monet's Old Age

Happy Birthday Monet!

Monet loved to eat good food. He sure didn't have to eat just beans anymore! On his birthday, he liked a special cake called *vert-vert*, which means green-green. The cake was colored with spinach!

YUCK

I read that Monet loved scones, which are like sweet biscuits. I love scones, too. Here's my grandma's recipe ↘

I get Grandma to help me with the oven.

SCONES   makes 10

Preheat oven 425°

2 cups flour
3 Tbsp. sugar
½ tsp. baking soda
½ tsp. salt
2 tsp. baking powder
} Mix

½ stick butter, cut up
½ cup milk with 4 Tbsp. vinegar added.
1 egg
Beat milk + egg together.

Cut butter into dry mix with 2 knives until it looks like big crumbs. Add milk/egg mix. Mix quickly. Knead dough on floured surface 5-6 times. Pat flat to ¾" thick. Cut with floured 2" round cutter. Bake on greased cookie sheet 15± minutes. Serve with jam + butter.

YUM!

When he was 68, Claude noticed that he was beginning to lose his sight. It got worse and worse. Claude was going blind.

Then Alice died in 1911. They had been together for thirty years. Claude was so upset he swore he would never paint again. Poor Claude! He did try to paint again, but finally, his eyesight was so bad he couldn't paint anymore. Then, in 1923, Claude had eye operations and got special glasses so he could see a little. I'm glad, because in the next few years he did some BEAUTIFUL paintings. They were called his *Decorations*.

Monet in 1923. © Roger-Viollet, Paris

This is Monet in his studio in 1923.

The Grand Finale

By his 83rd birthday, Claude had finished 22 giant paintings of waterlilies. Now they are in museums. I hope I can see them in person some day.

This is a picture of my paintbrush. It's a lot like one Monet used.

Monet painted with oil paints.

Waterlilies: Morning with Weeping Willows, 1914-18 (right section), by Claude Monet.
Musee del'Orangerie, Paris, France/Bridgeman Art Library

"When you go out to paint, try to forget what objects you have before you, a tree, a house, a field or whatever. Just think, here's a little square of blue, here's an oblong of pink, here's a streak of yellow, and paint it just as it looks to you, the exact color and shape ..." —Claude

On December 5, 1926, Claude Monet died. He was 86. He had been happy and sad, poor and rich. In his life, Monet painted more than 2,000 paintings. Now they sell for millions of dollars. They are worth it.

Steven, I hope that you like school more than Monet did! And I hope you get to see some of his water lilies one day, too. (If you go to New York City, you can see some at the Museum of Modern Art.) I'm not sure about the picture you did of me, but you did a great job on this report!

Ms. Brandt